SERGIO SERNA

THAT QUINCE WEEKEND

Joker & the Queen
PUBLISHING

CONTENTS

For every cousin who felt like a brother or sister,
for every family that stayed strong even when life got
messy.
For the nights we cruised with the windows down,
the laughter that echoed louder than the music,
and the memories we'll keep like treasures.

THE BURST PIPE

The pipe burst first. A violent crack fractured the silence of the upstairs wall, followed by the relentless hiss of water forcing its way into daylight. Spray arced across Mackenzie Sarabia's bedroom, streaking the hardwood like silver threads and drenching the rug until it darkened in spreading stains. The stream struck the quinceañera dress that hung with reverence on the closet door, flattening the once-proud folds of fabric. The gown sagged pitifully, embroidery wilting under the assault, each bead and stitch losing its delicate shimmer.

By the time Mack opened the door, the damage was already done.

Her scream tore through the Sarabia household with such intensity that even the dog downstairs barked in alarm, nails scrambling on tile as if ready to answer the call. Fifteen-year-old Mack was not simply crying for help; she was issuing a declaration of catastrophe, a shriek that could have summoned neighbors to the porch and priests to prayer.

"Oh my God! Mom! Dad! It's an emergency! HELP!"

Her pulse hammered as she stood frozen in the doorway, eyes locked on the ruin before her. The dress, her dress, selected after weeks of fittings, sharp disagreements, and whispered prayers, hung defeated under the merciless stream. She had pictured this night in vivid detail: herself gliding into the venue, the gown catching the light like moonlit silk, her friends cheering, her cousins smirking with envy, her parents beaming with pride. She had imagined a flawless scene: no wrinkles, no smudges, no interruptions. And now, mere hours before the doors would open, that vision drowned beneath the torrent of a broken pipe.

Her parents arrived in a rush. Gaby smelled faintly of sautéed onions and garlic, a scent that clung from the kitchen she had abandoned. Her dark hair, clipped back in haste, had slipped loose around her face, yet her striking features, so often compared to a younger Salma Hayek, commanded attention even in disarray. Sergio skidded in behind her, socks sliding across the wood, his expression caught between disbelief and outright panic. He looked like a man who had sprinted into a nightmare he had no script for.

"What's... wro..." he began, his voice faltering as his eyes met the drenched dress.

"Oh, snap."

Mack's chest rose and fell in shallow bursts. "My dress! It's ruined! The party is tonight, and—and—" Her voice fractured, splitting into sobs that hollowed her chest.

Before despair consumed her, Gaby wrapped her arms around Mack with the authority of a general and the tenderness of a mother. "Mija, breathe. In and out. The dress is not ruined. Wet, yes. Ruined, no. We will fix this." Her words carried the practiced calm she had used on night terrors and scraped knees, a voice that steadied storms. She smoothed Mack's hair and pressed her cheek against her daughter's temple. "You will still look beautiful tonight. I promise."

"That's not the point!" Mack jerked back, her face blotchy and her voice cutting sharp. "Everything has to be perfect. This is supposed to be my night, and now—"

"Now," Sergio interrupted, his tone lighter than hers yet edged with certainty, "you're forgetting who you're related to."

Both Gaby and Mack turned toward him. He stepped deliberately around the puddle, leaned against the doorframe, and folded his arms. "This family has never had a quince that went smoothly. Honestly, Mack, I was beginning to think yours was suspiciously calm."

Mack scowled. "How is that supposed to help?"

"Because it means you're still on track," Sergio answered. "If the worst we face is a busted pipe and a soggy hem, you're practically blessed. Trust me, I've witnessed disasters that made this look like a dress rehearsal."

Her mind spiraled in panic. What if this ruins everything? What if the photographs are wrecked? What if my cousins laugh for years? What if every holiday this story gets dragged out like a bad joke? Fear pressed on her chest until breathing felt like labor. She could already imagine the smirks, the teasing, the whispers that her quince had dissolved into a comedy of errors.

Her thoughts drifted to her abuela's words, stories she had once dismissed as melodrama. Every Sarabia girl gets tested, her grandmother had whispered with a knowing smile. The quince is not just a party. It is the storm you learn to walk through. Mack had rolled her eyes then, but now, with water staining the gown meant to crown her, she wondered if abuela had known something deeper.

A thunder of footsteps shook the hall. Mack's three best friends burst into the room, cheeks flushed from the playlist thumping downstairs.

"What happened?" one shrieked. Their gazes landed on the soaked gown.

Another scream ricocheted through the walls.

The girls clutched one another as if a boy band had materialized in front of them. Sergio winced, rubbing his ear. "If I closed my eyes," he muttered, "I'd swear NSYNC just announced a reunion tour. Or whichever group's poster is plastered on these walls now."

The friends ignored him, diving into chaotic improvisation.

"Blow dryer!"

"No, fans—lots of fans!"

"Don't touch it, you'll stretch the fabric!"

"Somebody get Febreze!"

One sprinted to the bathroom and returned with a tower of towels, tossing them into the puddle like sandbags against a flood. Another slammed into Mack's chair, sending it spinning into the wall. A third paced the room like a commander, waving her arms and issuing orders no one followed.

The bedroom transformed into a circus. The smell of damp fabric clashed with garlic clinging to Gaby's sleeves and the syrupy perfume one friend had over-applied. Mack's chest tightened as if the air itself pressed against her ribs.

Her friends were loyal, yes, but their loyalty now suffocated. One knelt too close to the dress, another nearly slipped across the slick floor, and the third sobbed almost as loudly as Mack herself. Voices rose in dissonance, each one competing with the hiss of the pipe.

Two older cousins materialized in the doorway, drawn by the noise.
"What's going on in here?" one asked, eyes widening at the spray. His grin spread slowly. "Ohhh, Mack. Not the dress!"

The other doubled over, gripping the doorframe for balance. "Girl, you didn't even make it to the church yet, and you're already trending in this house."

"Stop!" Mack snapped, her cheeks burning hot.

They raised their hands in mock innocence. "We're just saying, you can't spell quinceañera without chaos. It's tradition."

The room erupted again, friends shrieked louder, cousins howled, Gaby pressed her lips into a reluctant smile. Chaos piled onto Mack's shoulders until she thought she might collapse under its weight.

In her mind she replayed the photographs she had practiced: her standing beneath the chandelier at the venue, her smile perfected in the mirror, the angle rehearsed until flawless. She thought of the waltz drilled with her court, her toes pinched raw by new shoes. All of it meant to shine. Now she saw only water creeping toward the satin at her feet.

And it wasn't shallow vanity. The quinceañera marked more than a birthday. It was passage, heritage, a family's promise lived out in lace and music. She imagined her tias whispering judgments, recalling which girl carried herself with grace and which stumbled. She remembered her mother's luminous eyes the day they chose the dress. Mack wanted to rise to all of it, but at this pace she would leave behind only laughter.

Sergio clapped once, the sharp crack like a referee's whistle. The room stilled, save for the hiss of water.

"Alright," he said, voice steady. "Everybody calm down. Mack, mija, especially you. This isn't the end of your night. It's tradition."

Mack blinked. "A what?"

"A tradition," Sergio repeated with a grin. "This family has never had a quince that didn't explode in spectacular fashion. Yours was running too smooth. That's not who we are."

The cousins nodded, one even muttering, "Facts."

"Dad," Mack snapped, her voice pitching higher, "this is not the time for one of your stories!"

But Sergio held firm, arms crossed, eyes gleaming with mischief and affection. "It's exactly the time. Because if you don't hear what happened at your Tía Jessica's quince back in 1996, you'll keep believing this is the worst disaster ever. And trust me," he glanced at Gaby, who smirked knowingly, "it's not even close."

Her friends leaned forward, curiosity replacing panic. "Wait... what happened?" one whispered.

The cousins perked up, eyes wide like kids at a campfire. "Oh man," one said. "He's finally telling the Jessica story."

Mack crossed her arms, feigning disinterest though her voice cracked. "I don't care," she muttered, eyes locked on her father.

Sergio chuckled. "Sure you don't. But once you hear it, you'll realize a busted pipe is nothing compared to that weekend."

He let the room breathe, the dripping pipe keeping time like a metronome. Then, with casual authority, he gestured toward the cousins. "You two, outside with me for a second."

They exchanged glances, then obeyed, voices fading as the door clicked shut.

Mack hugged her arms around herself, fighting the rush of her thoughts. Gaby crouched by the bed, her voice hushed but unwavering. "We'll figure this out, mija. There's always a way. You are not alone in this."

Mack nodded, her throat tight. She looked again at the sodden hem, already imagining guests whispering about mishaps. Yet another thought pressed through: maybe every Sarabia quince carried chaos. Maybe perfection had never been the point. Maybe survival was.

Her eyes shifted to her friends, still buzzing with leftover adrenaline, and she allowed a shaky laugh. They would never abandon her. Her cousins might tease but would rally. Her parents were already plotting solutions. She realized then that no matter how chaotic the night became, she would not face it alone.
She drew in a breath, unsteady, but steadier than before.

And just like that, Mack's night bent toward another story, one born nearly thirty years earlier, on a weekend her family would never forget.

THE BELL RINGS

The bedroom pulsed with chaos, a storm that refused to settle, as towels smacked the hardwood in frantic slaps and skidded across the spreading puddle as if they could dam a river by insistence alone; a chair, shoved aside, crashed into the wall and rattled; Mack's best friends shouted over one another, their voices colliding like bumper cars until sense disappeared beneath the noise; her cousins lounged in the doorway like hecklers at a boxing match, tossing jokes that stung more than they helped, while Mack stood frozen at the center with her arms cinched around her ribs and the air pressing on her chest until she could hardly breathe, the quinceañera dress drooping beside her like a wounded soldier, its hem soaked and whispering disaster.

Sergio reappeared in the doorway, his stillness cutting cleanly through the uproar as he took in the wreckage, the towels and chairs and frantic teenagers, then crossed the slick floor with deliberate steps; his shoes squeaked, a calm counterpoint to the storm, and when he leaned close to Gaby and murmured something, her shoulders softened and her mouth curved into a grin, small but steadying, a lighthouse beam in fog.

"Alright, besties," Gaby said, clapping once, the sound cracking like a starter pistol. "We have work to do. Honey, you stay with Mack, you always know how to calm her down. And me?" She glanced at her outfit and smirked. "I am far too well dressed to stand ankle deep in a puddle."

The girls laughed despite themselves, the cousins tried not to, and the panic thinned just enough to let people breathe; Gaby seized that sliver of calm and used it, her voice bright but firm as she waved them toward the hall and said, "Come on, I need your help," and they filed out whispering questions while the hallway swallowed their voices, the cousins twitching to follow until Sergio lifted one hand without even looking and they obeyed the silent order, slinking away and pulling the door nearly shut so that a quieter hush followed, thin and trembling, punctuated only by the steady drip of water from the broken pipe.

Mack stared at the dress, the hem sagging and heavy with water, mocking every plan she had shaped in her head as she tried to imagine it restored, bright and whole, an image that would not hold no matter how she forced it; her throat tightened and her chest burned as if she had screamed without sound.

"No one is abandoning you," Sergio said softly, his voice carrying the kind of steadiness that makes the heart trust before the mind agrees as he stepped closer, choosing his footing with care. "They are doing their part in another room, and right now my part is here."

She nodded, thinly.

"Good," he said, crouching until their eyes met. "Fear is allowed, and anger too, but this night is not finished, not for this family; we do not stop because water tried to write another story."

Her gaze flicked to the dress. "What if I do not want a story," she said.

"That is the thing about stories," Sergio replied with a faint smile, "they show up whether we want them or not, and they do not leave until they have done their work; let me tell you about your Tía Jessica."

Mack did not answer, yet she did not resist; Sergio tugged the desk chair closer and sat, resting his hands on his knees as he drew a measured breath and began with the careful cadence of someone unwrapping memory: "San Jose, summer of nineteen ninety six; the Sarabia house on a Friday afternoon was never quiet, it was a concert hall, music pouring from every car and porch and cracked window; a cousin's ride shook with 'Latin Active,' the bass so deep it rattled the curb; another car blasted 'Back to the Hotel,' a NorCal anthem we claimed like a flag; down the block, someone floated 'Summertime in the LBC,' smooth and gold, while a truck rolled by booming 'California Love'; and somewhere, always, an uncle leaned into 'La Raza' as if it were gospel, the neighborhood turning into a single mixtape, each hook bleeding into the next and calling us home."

His eyes unfocused for a second, as if he could hear it again, before he added, "But that weekend did not begin on the street; it started in a classroom with me chained to a clock."

He leaned back, his tone slipping into the past. "Seventeen years old, stuck in English Literature and pretending to edit an essay while the second hand crawled; the room smelled like pencil shavings and chalk dust, a fan clicked in the corner and moved no air, sunlight stretched across the whiteboard and snared on a curled map of the world that had hung there too long; Mr. Alvarez walked the aisles with a stack of essays tucked beneath his arm, his voice deliberate, each word weighed like gold."

Sergio lifted one hand as though sketching the bar of light. "'Focus on your edits,' he said, 'precision is a kindness to your reader,' and he set my paper on the desk with marked margins and a small check by the thesis; he meant to encourage me, but all I could see was the clock, so I tapped my pencil and bounced my leg and rewrote a sentence and added a comma and deleted a word, bargaining with time."

Mack's shoulders eased by a fraction. "What were you writing about," she asked.

"Responsibility," he answered. "We had to describe a choice we felt proud of; I wrote about being the oldest son in a big family and how responsibility does not ask permission; it is a jacket you are handed whether it fits or not, and at first it hangs heavy and awkward and then it keeps you warm, and eventually you realize you would freeze without it," he said, smiling. "Mr. Alvarez probably did not expect wardrobe metaphors on a Friday."

She almost laughed, and the sound steadied her.

"Anyway," Sergio continued, "three o'clock was the door to freedom, and I counted every second on the way there," he said, letting the pipe serve as a metronome while Mack tucked her feet beneath her and watched him. "What was the plan," she asked, and I counted on my fingers: basketball at the park with the primos, that court with straight nets and clean paint where Mr. Carranza sat on the bench with his radio and cheered for whoever was losing; then cruising Story and King, windows down and music up, chrome catching the streetlights; after that, checking every last detail for Jessica's quince with your grandparents, the tables and centerpieces and food, the entrances and exits, the sound system; it was a lot, but it was our kind of lot."

His hands settled again. "And if the universe handed me one clean minute, I planned to ask my crush to prom."

Mack leaned forward. "Who," she said, and he only smiled. "A good story saves its reveal."

"In that classroom I kept forcing myself to care about one more sentence, though I was already outside in my head; I could hear sneakers on asphalt and bass lines thumping across the lot, and I could see my cousins leaning on their cars, talking with their hands and laughing like the weekend had already started," he said. "Mr. Alvarez stopped by again and said, 'You are restless today, Sergio, big plans,' and I told him, 'Family plans,' and he nodded and said, 'Then make your words carry their share; a clean sentence shows respect,' and he tapped the margin and moved on."

"He was right," Sergio said, smiling at the memory, "especially about the small things."

Mack glanced at the damp hem. "That pipe did not show respect," she said; "no," Sergio answered, "pipes do not respect, people do; your mom and friends are proving that in the hall, and your cousins will prove it next, and we are not finished."

She drew a breath that finally reached the bottom of her lungs, and the knot inside her chest loosened.

"Two fifty six," Sergio said; "four minutes to freedom; the room hummed with impatience, pens clicked, a girl folded a note with military precision, a boy whispered about catching his ride; outside, a mower droned and the smell of cut grass slid through the vents, and even the world seemed to hold its breath."

"What about the music," Mack asked; "you said people were blasting it," and Sergio grinned. "Always; Fridays in that lot were a contest; one car shook with 'Latin Active,' another with 'Back to the Hotel,' someone else floated 'Summertime in the LBC'; you could not escape 'California Love,' and sooner or later an uncle would play 'La Raza' like an anthem; every car fought to claim the weekend soundtrack."

He traced an invisible clock. "Two fifty seven; two fifty eight; I underlined a verb that mattered and finished my thought, and it clicked into place; for a heartbeat I forgot time existed and then the minute turned; two fifty nine."

Mack listened to the pipe, which no longer sounded like a threat so much as a timekeeper.

"I closed my notebook," Sergio said, "slid the pencil into the spiral, and looked up; Mr. Alvarez wore the smile teachers use when they know the bell, not their lecture, will be the last word."

He glanced around Mack's room as if overlaying desks on the space. "A bell can open a door you have been pushing against all day, and when it rang I told myself to move with purpose, because the weekend had work for me."

"What kind of work," she asked, and he answered, "the invisible kind, the kind nobody claps for but everybody needs: straightening chairs, smoothing tablecloths, reminding Tía Alma to sit before her legs gave out, sending little cousins to the yard so the cake would not melt, checking microphone batteries and keeping a drawer full of extras, and keeping lists in my pocket and in my grandfather's wallet and under the chili magnet on the fridge."

Mack's mouth twitched. "The chili magnet," she said, and he nodded. "You have seen it; it is still there."

He breathed in and let the air go slowly. "In those last seconds before the bell I thought about my grandparents and about Jessica, who had practiced her waltz until her toes blistered, and about the question I still wanted to ask; it made my stomach drop like the first plunge on a roller coaster; fear and excitement feel the same inside, and the difference is what you do next."

The pipe dripped; laughter drifted from the hallway, faint but steady, and Mack pictured her friends finding a fan, a drying rack, maybe a joke that made the work lighter.

"Two fifty nine and thirty seconds," Sergio said; "the last stretch; someone coughed; Mr. Alvarez eyed the clock as if he might bargain with it and then surrendered; he stacked his papers and said, 'Good work, people, use your weekend well.'"

"In our family," he added, voice softened, "that was never just advice; it was instruction, and it meant you belonged to something larger than nerves."

Mack leaned forward, looser now, her voice clear. "What happened next," she asked, and he answered, "the bell rang, three o'clock, the hallway burst into life, footsteps and laughter and lockers slamming, and I moved with the crowd but I was not drifting, because I had a list to follow and a promise to keep and a question waiting for its moment."

Silence settled again, yet it felt comfortable, the echo of that bell hanging in the room and braiding with the slowing drip of water.

"In that moment," he said, "I was proud to be a Sarabia, not because things went right but because we showed up for one another when they did not," and he looked from Mack to the damp dress and added, "and that is exactly what is happening here."

Mack swallowed and lifted her eyes. "So the bell is ringing here too," she said; "it is," Sergio answered.

The house had softened; footsteps rustled in the hall; the door cracked open and Gaby peeked in, her smile bright with triumph, and said, "We have a plan: better towels, a drying rack, an extra fan; we are moving the dress, and we are going to save it."

Mack imagined the photos again, and this time the image held; if the tías whispered later, let them; let them say the girl did not fold; let them say the dress nearly drowned and still shined; she straightened without thinking, her spine remembering itself, and her eyes met her parents' as the knot in her chest loosened another turn.

"Okay," she said, and Gaby echoed, "okay; Sergio, stay with her; chicas, with me," her voice already drifting into the hallway and carried by the rhythm of busy feet.

Sergio squeezed Mack's hand. "Ready for the rest," he asked, and she nodded. "After the bell," she said, "start there," and he promised, "we will," before he looked once more at the pipe and the dress and his daughter, steadier now, and the room no longer felt like a disaster so much as a beginning, a story waiting to be told; the drip slowed and then stopped, as if even the plumbing understood that the bell had already rung.

KEYS TO THE VAN

The van waited in the sun like a relic that refused to retire. A 1994 Ford Econoline, beige and boxy, its paint dull from years of weather and weekend missions. The seats bore the record of our family history: soda stains fossilized in fabric, crumpled burrito wrappers wedged between cushions, the faint, eternal scent of taco truck grease clinging to every vent. Even the air inside seemed layered—carne asada smoke, salt from fries, and the ghost of strawberry soda that refused to fade.

On good days, the van was a stage. On hard days, it was a confessional. Today, it was both. Jessica sat in the passenger seat, her reflection steady in the window, but I knew the difference between confidence and armor.

To me, that van was freedom and burden wrapped in metal. Freedom, because it meant independence. Burden, because it made me the family chauffeur. In a Sarabia household, a driver's license wasn't a privilege—it was conscription. With keys came duty, and duty didn't negotiate. Every mile whispered expectation. Every pickup was a reminder that being the oldest meant carrying weight no one else would.

That Friday was no exception. I left English Lit still tasting the stale air of the classroom, my notebook warm from scribbles, my head replaying the face of a crush I hadn't dared name aloud. The idea of prom drifted somewhere between fantasy and punctuation. I'd written words I didn't expect anyone to read, metaphors that probably didn't make sense to anyone but me. But I believed in language the way some people believed in luck—it had weight, it could shift air, it could build worlds.

Jessica was waiting outside my class, exactly where I knew she'd be, leaning against the wall with her comadres orbiting her like satellites. Their laughter cut through the hallway noise. She spotted me before I spoke.

"Driver," she said, arms crossed. "We need a ride."

I raised an eyebrow. "Do I look like a taxi?"

"You look like my brother," she said sweetly. "Which makes you my driver."

Her friends laughed. One whispered loud enough for everyone to hear, "His van smells like tacos."

"Correction," I said, sliding open the heavy door. "It smells like generations of tacos. Show some respect."

The comadres groaned but climbed in anyway. Jessica took the passenger seat, claiming it like a throne she'd earned by birthright. I caught her smirk in the rearview mirror and rolled my eyes, though the corners of my mouth gave me away.

This was our rhythm—sarcasm as affection, teasing as a dialect. Some siblings fought. We sparred in sentences. She was the golden child. I was the reluctant narrator. Together, we made the noise that held our family's shape.

Wild 94.9 buzzed to life when I turned the ignition. The speakers crackled, then settled into the steady voice of St. John, his banter smooth as a late-afternoon breeze. He promised the weekend's hottest mix, and for once, I believed him. Jessica twisted the volume knob until the bass made the cupholders tremble.

"This is the soundtrack," she said.

"The soundtrack to what?" I asked. "You talking nonsense with your friends?"

"The soundtrack to my quince weekend," she said, her grin wide and certain. "And you better not forget it."

Her tone shifted when she added, "As long as Erick and Billy keep their distance, nothing can ruin this."

She tried to make it a joke, but the names landed heavy. I wanted to swear thunder on anyone who hurt her, but all I said was, "It'll be fine," hoping the words could hold.

"You'd better hope Wild plays a slow jam," I said, forcing levity. "Your waltz could use divine intervention."

She laughed, and the comadres followed, their laughter echoing through the van like music itself.

Driving the Sarabia van always carried an unspoken sermon about duty. Our parents didn't have to explain it; it was the air we breathed. Grades, respect, work ethic—that was our trinity. They didn't want riches; they wanted stability. Jessica's burden was her quince. Mine was the van. Different tasks, same inheritance.

"So what's the plan?" she asked, tying her hair into a ponytail, her bracelets chiming like a warning.

"Drop you and your fan club off," I said. "Then pick up the primos. If I don't, they'll still be arguing over who owes who for last week's tacos."

The comadres howled. Jessica shook her head. "You love it," she said. "Don't lie. You live for being the one with the keys."

"Keys are heavy," I said. "Everybody wants a ride. Nobody wants to buy gas."

She laughed. "You sound like Dad."

"I'll take that as a threat," I said. "Keep it up and I'll invoice you for emotional labor and air fresheners."

She grinned, leaning back as we rolled down the street, Wild 94.9 matching the hum of the tires. For a moment, everything felt weightless—siblings, sunlight, music, possibility. Yet beneath the laughter, I could feel the pressure of what waited. Quinceañeras weren't parties.

They were declarations. In our family, success wasn't personal; it was shared. So was failure.

Jessica looked out the window, her reflection flickering in rhythm with the passing palm trees. "Pick up the pace," she said. "We need to stop at home before your sweaty art session."

"Basketball is not sweaty," I said. "It's poetry in motion."

"So art smells like socks?" she asked.

The van erupted again, laughter rising like heat.

"Real art leaves a mark," I said. "Sometimes it's beautiful, sometimes it stinks. But it lingers."

Jessica gave me a look halfway between amusement and admiration. "You're ridiculous," she said, but her voice had softened.

The afternoon light spilled through the windshield like a benediction. Palm trees sliced the sky, jasmine tangled with exhaust, and every radio in the Bay seemed to pulse with the same beat. Friday had arrived, loud and unapologetic.

In my mind, I mapped the next stops—the primos. Jeff would be combing his hair. Moi would still be flexing at a mirror. Ricky would be locked in a bathroom debate with his reflection. Beto would be inventing noise. Robert would trip over nothing. And Katy—the lone prima who matched us stride for stride—would cut them all down with one well-placed line.

Jessica caught me smiling. "What's funny?"

"The lineup," I said. "We could make trading cards. Six disasters, one limited edition set."

Jessica laughed so hard she nearly cried. "Who's who?"

"Jeff's the rookie who thinks he's the MVP. Moi's the heart-throb card—mirror finish. Ricky's limited edition, bathroom break included. Beto's holographic and guaranteed to annoy. Robert's card falls out of the pack before you open it. And Katy? She's the chase card no one can handle."

The comadres cackled. Jessica shook her head, wiping her eyes. "You should write that down."

"Maybe I will," I said.

"You always say that," she teased.

"Maybe one day I'll mean it."

The van slowed at a red light. I watched a man in the car next to us nod along to the same station, the same song. It struck me that half the Bay was tuned to this frequency—different cars, same rhythm. That was the magic of stories. They connected strangers through invisible threads.

The light turned green. Jessica leaned toward the mirror, frowning at a stray strand. "Hurry up," she said. "We need time to fix our faces."

"You act like we're driving to a magazine shoot."

"We are," she said, her confidence absolute. "A quince is basically a runway."

I laughed, shaking my head. The van jolted over a pothole, rattling its frame like a drum solo. We turned onto Jeff's street and parked at the curb.

Behind me, the comadres whispered plans for makeup and outfits, their voices tumbling over one another in a familiar melody. Jessica stretched her arms and gave me a knowing smile.

"You ready?" she asked.

"Always," I said, though it came out like a prayer.

The door to Jeff's house opened. A silhouette filled the frame. The first primo. The chaos was waiting.

The weekend had officially begun.

THE LINEUP

The van rattled down familiar streets, its tired engine grumbling like it was already exhausted by the weekend ahead. A few minutes earlier the back seats had buzzed with Jessica's comadres; now it was just me, the hum of Wild 94.9 dissolving into static, and empty cushions waiting for cousins who never traveled light. The task sounded simple and felt heavy: collect the roster, one stop at a time, and roll to the court as a single, noisy unit. Every stop added more than bodies. It added history, a new layer of noise, another memory welded to the van.

First up was Jeff. I honked twice. He stumbled out with hair in every direction and eyes half closed like he had crawled out of a cave. He wore swagger the way some people wore a jacket: confidently, even when it did not fit. Jeff believed he was the MVP even when his shirt was inside out. He had heart, no doubt, but he covered nerves with big talk. Loud dreams, shaky execution, always ready to lace up. I envied the way he trusted his own myth. Sometimes belief carries a person farther than a clean stat line.

"Bout time," he muttered as he climbed in. "We winning today. Watch."

"Brush your teeth first?" I asked, leaning away.

"Gatorade fixes everything," he said, grinning wide enough to sell the idea.

Next was Ricky. True to form, he sprinted out the door with a folded newspaper under one arm and his laces untied, already living inside a minor emergency. Ricky had a gift for finding the nearest bathroom at the worst possible moment. He tripped on the last step, caught himself, then waved like it was choreographed.

"Shotgun!" he yelled, making a move for the front.

"Not happening," I said without looking. "Back seat."

"Man, you're harsh," he sighed, flopping down and immediately rummaging through Jeff's backpack for snacks he had not bought.

Moi waited against his fence, comb in hand, fade sharp enough to catch sunlight. He was not just a mirror. He was a problem. Smooth handle, quiet footwork, jumper like a promise. If Jeff was belief, Moi was follow-through. He slid into the van with a nod and a look that said score first, talk later.

"Finally," he said. "Time to remind the city who runs these courts."

"Your mirror," I said, tipping my chin toward his pocket.

"And the scoreboard," he answered, not missing a beat.

Next came the siblings, Beto and Katy, side by side as always, opposite in every way that mattered and somehow perfectly paired. Beto started talking before he reached the curb.

"Sergio, this van is a biohazard. Ricky, you fall yet today? Jeff, you still ugly?"

Insults were oxygen to him. The louder he roasted, the more he cared. He never said I love you; he showed it by keeping you in range.

Katy did not waste words. She marched to the passenger door, opened it, and looked at Ricky. "Move."

"I called shotgun," he protested.

"Shotgun does not count when I am here," she said, sliding in with quiet authority. No one argued. Katy was balance to the boys' chaos. She made everything sharper without raising her voice.

The last door thudded shut. Noise bloomed. Jeff teased Moi about his comb. Ricky asked whether Katy planned to cross him in front of everyone again. Beto leaned forward and shouted, "So how's Jessica holding up? That dress dry yet, or we still calling it the SpongeBob special?"

Katy rolled her eyes, a smile tugging anyway. "Shut up, Beto. You know you cry first when she comes down those stairs."

"Facts," Jeff said. "She's the star this weekend."

Ricky nodded. "Quince only comes once. Gotta be perfect."

"Perfect is overrated," Moi said, like he was narrating a shoe commercial. "She just needs to own it."

Under the teasing lived something solid. That was us. Nobody escaped a joke, but beneath the noise sat pride and a loyalty that did not need speeches.

We rolled east, the van now heavier with bodies and energy. First stop: cheap gas on Julian and Thirty-third. Ritual mattered. Cracked pavement, gum welded to the pump, a coffee smell that never matched the taste. I filled the tank while the cousins heckled each other through the glass. Moi checked his reflection. Jeff bragged about a dunk he would swear he landed whether he did or not. Ricky clutched his stomach like fumes could trigger disaster. Beto shot at anyone in range. Katy leaned back, cracking sunflower seeds, unimpressed by all of us.

"Only station cheaper than this," I said when I climbed back in, "is the one in your imagination."

Next stop: 7-Eleven. No game began without Gatorade and something salty. Back then you were not legit unless you walked onto the blacktop with a cold bottle sweating in your hand. We borrowed swagger from television and tried to graft it onto our streets.

Inside, Ricky grabbed chips like he was preparing for winter. Moi reached for lemon-lime, cracked it open like a trophy, then grabbed a second for later. Jeff argued about nickels with the cashier, convinced the register had cheated him. Katy paid fast and waited by the door, opening another pack of seeds. Beto planted himself in front of the cooler and announced to the store, "Only scrubs drink orange Gatorade. Winners go lemon-lime."

"Get out of the way," Moi said, nudging him aside. "Nobody is listening to you."

"Except me," Ricky answered, lifting a fruit punch like a championship belt. "Real men drink red."

"Real men make it to halftime without running off the court," Jeff said, and the cousins cackled. The cashier sighed the sigh of a person trapped in a teen movie.

We spilled back outside with sugar and salt stacked in our arms. Beto opened his chips before the door closed and wore crumbs like a badge. Jeff still mourned a few missing cents. Moi balanced bottles like he had a game plan. Ricky tucked a pack of donuts into his pocket like contraband. Katy said nothing and saw everything.

We turned into the park as the sun angled low. Our rivals were already there. Donald laughed too hard at every line Billy Ho delivered. Billy strutted like the court had a deed with his name on it. Erick looked past us toward the street as if Jessica might appear out of nowhere. She was home, busy with her comadres, thinking about hair and flowers, not Erick's shot selection. That truth soured his face.

We checked the ball. Game on.

Moi set the tone. Dribble, shift, rise, net. Clean, like a metronome. Katy matched the beat and then changed it. One hard step, a cross that clipped daylight, a layup that kissed the glass. Jeff tried to live up to his own press release and delivered comedy instead, which had its place. Ricky hustled for two possessions and then vanished toward the bathrooms, which also had its place. Beto filled every pause with noise.

"Billy, pass the ball before it melts your hands," he shouted.

"Better than watching Jeff miss another layup," Billy shot back.

"That is called intimidation," Jeff said, holding up his palms. "I meant to miss."

"Yeah," Moi laughed, draining another jumper, "you are scaring the backboard."

Donald tried to keep Katy in front of him and kept losing the argument with his feet.

"Stay on your toes," she said quietly after a layup. "You look like you are skating."

The court roared. Donald flushed. Erick's jaw set. He focused on Katy more than the ball, and when she crossed him clean, knees bending in a way that made the whole park wince, Beto made it a headline.

"Erick! She sent you to church. Go light a candle."

Erick swore under his breath and looked toward the street again. The look said starve me out and see what happens. It made the air sharper.

The score climbed. The talk got louder. Moi hit a step-back that felt personal. Katy tipped a pass to herself, then stuck the layup. Jeff celebrated a rebound like he had won a trophy. Ricky reappeared, winded and suspiciously empty-handed. Beto never stopped. The court became a stage, pride balanced on the rim.

Game point. Moi pulled from midrange and held the follow-through. Net. Katy sealed it with a stop that felt like a door closing. We dapped up like champions and let the noise swell. The joy carried heat but it carried something heavier too. Respect was in the air, and so was the lack of it. Rivalry had grown teeth.

Erick did not look at Katy. He looked past us, searching for a girl who was not there, and then back at us like the absence was our fault. When she crossed him, his pride hit the asphalt first. That was the part he could not shake.

The sun slid low and painted the court gold. Sneakers scraped. Bottles clinked. Somebody's radio drifted through with a snippet of "Back to the Hotel," then snapped to static. The sounds folded into evening. I felt the weight gather.

This was not just another win. It was a first spark.

We left the court loud on purpose, as if volume could hold a door shut. Pride is a poor mechanic. It tightens the wrong bolts and swears the wheels will not come off.

The weekend had only begun. The chisme was already writing itself.

COOL WATER AND CHAOS

The van rattled back into the driveway, its wheels crunching over gravel as the late afternoon light stretched into evening. The cousins spilled out, still sweaty and loud, voices bouncing off the house with leftover energy from our victory at the court. For hours, the blacktop had been our stage. Each shot, each roast, each laugh had added to the show. Now the house waited like a second arena, its own mix of rules, rivalries, and expectations.

Jessica and her comadres had already claimed her room, a muffled chorus of gossip, music, and laughter rising behind a closed door. That left the living room, kitchen, and hallways for the rest of us, and we filled them fast.

Before I could escape upstairs, Mom and Abuela intercepted me in the kitchen. They stood side by side like sentinels, commanding without needing to raise their voices. Mom touched my arm first, her smile gentle but her tone deliberate.

"You did good today, Sergio. Always making sure everyone's where they need to be. I see the man you're becoming."

Abuela nodded slowly, her gaze cutting straight through me. "You carry yourself with respect. That is everything."

Their approval warmed me, but it came with weight. Just as I turned to leave, Mom added, "Now if only you'd put that same energy into your college applications. Responsibility doesn't end in the driveway."

She wasn't wrong. What she didn't see was that I'd already started. My desk upstairs was covered in essays, envelopes, and application drafts written after midnight. I wasn't running from the future. I was pacing myself toward it. Her expectations weren't a chain, they were fuel. Still, her voice had a way of making me feel like I was always one step behind, chasing a finish line that kept moving.

Before I could answer, Jessica swept in from the hall. "Mom, Abuela, he smells like the court. If you want him to impress anyone tonight, let him shower before the wallpaper peels off."

Her timing was perfect. Both women laughed, clearing my path. Jessica shot me a wink, her silent "You owe me."

She tugged my sleeve before I disappeared. "Thanks for today. You always come through."

I shrugged it off. "Don't make it sound serious. I'm just doing my job."

Her grin softened into something genuine. "No, really. You've been holding everything together. You think we don't notice, but we do."

The words landed deeper than I expected. I masked it with humor. "Don't go soft on me now. You'll ruin your reputation."

She smirked, slipping back into armor. 'Fine. I'll save it for my speech when I'm running the world. Now hurry up before someone faints."

I wanted to joke back and couldn't. For a second, I saw her not as the star of the weekend but as my little sister, the one who used to fall asleep in the van after late grocery runs. I swallowed the lump in my throat and nodded. That was Jessica: quick, sharp, and unafraid of truth.

I stepped into the bathroom.

The water blasted against the tile, steam rising until the mirror disappeared. I always turned the heat up too high for anyone else to stand it. Back then, my showers looked like a Prince music video, steam swirling, lights catching the water just right, everything dramatic and over the top. By the time I stepped out, it felt like I'd shed the day's weight, reborn and ready to face whatever came next.

Then came the ritual. Fresh Jordans laced with care. Baggy jeans sagging just right. A Jordan spirit jersey snug across my shoulders. Three sprays of Cool Water cologne, never two, never four. That was the armor. You weren't ready until the scent followed you like a signature, faint but undeniable. I caught my reflection and grinned. The night was mine to claim.

Meanwhile, the living room had turned into its own circus. Moi and Robert were circling Jessica's friends like performers who believed their lines would land. Elena, the loud one, laughed at everything, fueling their confidence. Her friend was quieter, arms crossed, polite smile, not playing along. Moi leaned on the wall, comb gliding through his fade, grin rehearsed to perfection. Robert cracked jokes about falling during the game, pretending it was part of his plan. Elena laughed so hard she almost fell herself, but the quiet girl only raised one eyebrow. She wasn't dismissive, just powerful in her silence. Even then, I felt it.

Katy emerged from Jessica's closet wearing borrowed clothes that looked like they had always been hers. That was her gift, she didn't wear outfits; she owned them. Leaning in the doorway, cracking sunflower seeds, she shook her head at the scene. "Less drama, boys," she said, heading for the couch.

On the carpet, Ricky and Beto battled on the Genesis, Street Fighter II flashing across the screen. Controllers clicked like typewriters.

"Bro, you're garbage! I'm about to end you with one hand!" Ricky shouted.

"You couldn't end a tutorial," Beto fired back. "Watch this combo!"

Their trash talk climbed until the air itself buzzed. Then Abuela appeared. She didn't storm in. She didn't have to. She just stood in the doorway, hands on hips, presence enough to silence everyone.

Abuela always reminded us of Wonder Woman, the old-school one from TV. You could believe she could block bullets with bracelets, and if you doubted, the chancla in her hand erased all doubt.

The sandal launched like a missile, slicing the air and smacking Beto square on the head. He froze mid-word, controller in hand, and nodded like he'd just been reminded of the law of gravity.

The room stayed quiet for half a beat before laughter cracked through. Abuela shook her head, muttering about mouths that needed more soap than food. Nobody pushed back. Nobody ever did. Abuela had power, what kids now call rizz, and she didn't need a mic to command a room. One glare from her ended rebellion faster than any threat. Even Moi stood straighter. Even Beto learned silence, for thirty seconds.

Order returned. Moi and Robert kept working their charm on Jessica's friends. Katy lounged on the couch, spitting sunflower seed shells neatly into a paper cup. Ricky sulked, Beto rubbed his head, and I leaned against the wall, Cool Water still hanging in the air, my Jordans catching the last of the sunlight.

The court had only been the warm-up. The real show waited outside. Soon the streets would wake, headlights stretching across asphalt, bass shaking windows, engines rumbling like thunder. Cruising wasn't just entertainment. It was ritual. It was a declaration, a living story.

Out there, the night would be written not in ink but in motion: laughter spilling from open windows, music pulsing through car doors, chrome catching the glow of passing lights. Tonight wasn't about being seen. It was about being remembered.

As I looked around, at my cousins, at Jessica's friends, at Abuela watching from the hallway with that quiet pride, I knew the story had already begun. The next chapter waited just beyond the front door.

STORY AND KING

The van drew us in like filings to a magnet, each cousin snapping into place until the old Econoline thrummed with heat and motion again. Ricky came last, charging out of the kitchen with a foil-wrapped burrito the size of his forearm. He was already chewing before his second foot hit the driveway, cheeks full, eyes bright, laughter ready, the picture of a man who believed appetite was a competitive sport.

"Bro, seriously?" Moi slid into the back seat, shaking his head like the universe had once again proven his theory about Ricky. "You couldn't wait five minutes?"

"Energy food," Ricky mumbled through carne asada and salsa. "Champions eat first."

Katy settled into the passenger seat, cracking sunflower seeds with the rhythm of a metronome. "Champions also make it through the night," she said, and the van answered with laughter that rattled the cup holders.

That was how the night began, loud, messy, joyful. The kind of start that came with a warning label if you knew how to read it.

I told Mack, later, that this was the era of the pager. Pagers turned boys into messengers and messengers into problem solvers. If you got buzzed, you moved. If it flashed 911, you moved faster. We didn't live on screens we carried everywhere. We lived on numbers that blinked from a little rectangle clipped to our belts. Mine was a Motorola Bravo Express, glossy black, a miracle that could display letters as well as numbers. It felt futuristic until it buzzed in your pocket and reminded you that the future still needed a payphone.

You'd pat your jeans for quarters and find none, then start digging through the van, ashtray, cup holders, map pocket, looking for loose change while your responsibility waited somewhere in the dark. The system worked, just not conveniently. And that was the point I wanted Mack to hear. Life moved, but not at the tap of a thumb.

The stereo baptized the night. 2Pac's voice filled the cabin, heavy and holy, washing over the worn upholstery like smoke from an altar. It was spring of 1996, deep in the coastal rivalry that made radio feel like a war zone. Out here, he wasn't background music. He was weather. He was warning. He was pride.

We didn't yet know what September would steal from the West, but even now, I can still feel the chill of it coming. And behind that chill, the ache from the year before, when Selena's voice was silenced and kitchens across California went quiet for a week.

Those artists didn't just chart, they scored our lives. When they disappeared, the map changed.

Cruising in San Jose wasn't a joyride; it was a ritual. A moving congregation with its own loop, its own rules. Your paint could shine or your bumper could hang by faith and wire. If your car rolled, it belonged.

This was the city that gave birth to Lowrider Magazine, not trivia, testimony. The route lived in our bones.

Start at The Alameda, slide past the arena where the Sharks brought a new kind of faith to the city, drift as the street became Santa Clara, cut toward King Road, loop at Story, double back when headlights stretched too far. Some nights the cops ended the story early. Most nights they let it breathe, so long as we didn't give them a reason to turn the page. Cruising was technically illegal, but culturally inevitable.

The van wasn't pretty, but it was faithful. We merged into the river of cars, and the city responded with light. Headlamps became a necklace stretching in both directions. Bass rolled beneath us from other lanes. Somewhere, a lowrider floated on hydraulics like it had learned to breathe differently. Windows slid down. Greetings crossed in the air like birds. The night felt choreographed, not by one person, but by everyone together.

Inside our metal bubble, the roasting continued because that was ritual too. Jeff tapped the back of my seat, announcing that Ricky wouldn't survive until Story Road. Moi, ever the prophet, bet five bucks Ricky would vanish before the U-turn. Ricky swore his stomach was made of iron. Katy, calm and surgical, said iron rusted. The van needed a moment to savor that one.

Traffic slowed us into the rhythm that made cruising feel like a ceremony. Inch, rest, inch again, the Econoline rocking gently like the street was water. I tapped the door to the beat leaking from nearby cars. You didn't cruise to arrive. You cruised to belong.

Halfway down Santa Clara, the station changed. A voice slid over the static, low and smooth. "This is Big Daddy Victor Zaragoza, and you're tuned in to the Turnin' Off the Lights dedication show." The whole boulevard softened. People leaned closer. Engines hummed quieter. Even the street seemed to exhale.

And that's when I thought of her. Dream Girl. That's the only name I'll use here. Your mother knows the real one, she could say it in a heartbeat if she wanted to. As Big Daddy cued a slow jam, I told myself the weekend might have room for a conversation that mattered. All I needed was five quiet minutes between errands and rehearsals to ask a question that had been living in my chest for weeks. Maybe prom was the answer she'd consider. The music made it sound possible.

The van didn't allow deep thoughts for long. Jeff leaned forward and asked if Ricky needed a doctor or a priest. Ricky said he was fine, wiping sweat from his forehead. Beto announced that a volcanic event was imminent and told everyone to lift valuables off the floor. Moi counted down just to add drama, stopping at two because comedy lives there. Ricky told everyone to shut up. Katy smiled, which in our family meant she was having a great time.

The burrito had chosen violence. Ricky's body surrendered. His heel bounced. His eyes locked on the brake lights ahead as if he could part them by will alone. He made a low sound that could have been prayer. We were boxed in by chrome and steel, and it felt like a moral lesson in traffic: sometimes, you just have to endure.

He didn't. The sliding door rattled open, and Ricky bolted into the night with the speed of divine panic. "Hey!" I shouted, reaching for the door, but he was already gone, sprinting along the shoulder, arms pumping, destiny ahead, judgment behind.

Beto leaned halfway out, thrilled. "Hey everybody! Ricky's taking a steamy one!" he bellowed across lanes, voice cutting through bass and laughter. If he had a sash, it would have read Town Crier. If he had a bell, he would have rung it until Santa Clara Street applauded.

The van exploded with laughter. Even Katy broke, covering her mouth as if that could contain it. Some stories fade. Others follow a man to every barbecue for the rest of his life. This was the second kind.

Traffic demanded patience, so we rolled forward, our van a moving witness. By the time we made the U-turn and came back down the boulevard, Ricky was leaning against a light pole, chatting up two girls from his school with confidence he hadn't earned.

I rolled down the window. Beto beat me to it. "You wash your hands?" he shouted, loud enough to echo off the buildings. The girls burst into laughter. Ricky pointed at us, insulted but grinning, then climbed back into the van with the swagger of someone trying to renegotiate the narrative. In our family, you couldn't rewrite the story, but you could take your roast like a pro, and Ricky did.

A different kind of attention followed us after that. Men in neighboring cars tried to catch Katy's eye because thirst has always been brave. She ignored them with style. She liked our lane better. She knew our hearts, our habits, and the rule that saved her time: don't waste breath on simple fools. She cracked another round of seeds and looked ahead, reading the traffic lights like scripture.

The laughter had just faded into a comfortable hum when the pager at my hip buzzed. Three sharp bleats, then a pause, then three more. I looked down. The tiny screen glowed with the only code you never wanted to see from Pops: 911.

He could have written more, a time, a word, a place, but he didn't. Which told me everything I needed to know about urgency, and nothing about what waited.

I told Mack later that truth arrived differently that night. Pops didn't want to explain. He wanted us to witness. He needed the primos to see with our own eyes, so the lesson would live in our bones, not just in our memories. I didn't understand that yet. I only knew duty had climbed into the van and taken a seat beside fear.

While I stared at the pager, the cousins argued about whether Ricky's sprint counted as cardio. Moi said yes, provided he learned from it. Jeff said no, because lessons required humility. Ricky claimed his dignity was intact, which made everyone laugh again, because honesty is brave but delusion is funnier.

The road opened ahead. Pops's code still blinked. Somewhere between the laughter and the lowriders, the night had changed.

A rumor reached us first, a friend in the next lane shouting that familiar faces were gathering near the hall, faces that didn't belong at a quince unless the plan was trouble. The names matched our rivals from the court, the ones who didn't know how to lose quietly. The words dropped into my stomach like a stone into water, fast, cold, certain.

I let the van roll, thinking about timing, about how one bad idea can bloom into a dozen worse ones if you give it room. Pops wanted us at the hall now. The cousins were ready to turn any night into a mission if you gave them a reason. The city pulsed around us, headlights blinking like nerves.

Here is the part I didn't tell anyone until years later. If I had spoken differently on the court earlier that day, if we had celebrated with grace instead of fire, maybe none of this would have happened. Pride doesn't like to be ignored. It looks for an audience, and when it finds one, it performs. That's what I feared as the pager buzzed again. I feared that my mouth had invited the wrong kind of attention to my sister's night.

We eased out of the thickest part of traffic, the Econoline shaking at thirty and settling at thirty-five. The cousins quieted. The city still glowed behind us, the ritual of cruising looping on without us, music, lights, laughter. Inside, everything had shifted. Celebration had become mission. The night had sharpened.

I looked at the pager one last time, then at the road. I told Mack that this was the moment when story and responsibility braided so tightly together that I could feel the weave. Pops had called us. The rivals had chosen their stage. Jessica's night had become a test. And the hardest truth settled in my chest as we approached the hall: this might be the end of the weekend before it truly began, and it might be my fault.

THE WRITING ON THE WALL

By the time we pulled into the lot, it was already past eleven thirty—a detail that should have been the first warning that the night had turned against us. A hall on the eve of a quinceañera was supposed to glow with life: cousins darting in and out with crates of decorations, music humming through a cracked doorway, Pops pacing with his clipboard while Mom and Abuela directed tablecloths and flowers into place.

Instead, the block pulsed with red and blue light bouncing off brick walls. Two SJPD cruisers crouched at the curb, doors open, radios spitting fragments of static. The air reeked of aerosol and broken glass, sharp and metallic. Even before I cut the ignition, I knew the celebration had been gutted.

We stepped out slowly, our sneakers crunching over shards scattered like cruel confetti. Pops stood in the doorway, his fists clenched so tight his knuckles had gone white. His jaw worked

like he was chewing words too dangerous to release. When he finally spoke, his voice came low and steady, terrible in its calm.

"It's trashed. Windows. Walls. Look for yourself."

We obeyed, though the evidence screamed without guidance.
Windows gaped with jagged teeth. Spray paint dripped in thick
black and red lines, bleeding down the plaster like open wounds.
Tables lay overturned, chairs thrown aside, paper cups crushed
under careless feet. The dance floor—Jessica's stage—was
streaked with paint. Worst of all, scrawled across the outer wall in
arrogant loops, two names mocked us: Erick. Billy.

They hadn't just destroyed the hall. They had signed their
crime like a dare.

Jeff swore loud enough to echo across the block. Beto bounced
on his toes, fists twitching for a fight. Moi said nothing, his silence more dangerous than shouting. Ricky barked out a laugh
that wasn't laughter at all, just the sound of disbelief scraping its
way out.

Katy stepped forward, arms wide, voice sharp. "Stop. Don't
make this worse."

But rage listens to no one. One by one, the boys slipped past
her, sprinting into the night, swallowed by shadows and payback.
Katy's jaw locked tight, but instead of chasing them, she turned
toward Jessica, who was climbing out of a car with her friends.

That sight crushed me harder than the vandalism. Her comadres had been laughing a moment earlier, but the sound died
the second their eyes found the wall. Mom followed close, arms

crossed, face carved from stone. Abuela came last, her back straight and her chin high, radiating the kind of strength that refused to bow even now.

They took in the wreckage without a word. Silence pressed heavier than any scream.

Jessica's eyes locked on the graffiti, then on me. The fury there hollowed me out. "This is because of you," she said, her voice steady and lethal. "You had to start something with them. And now look. My quince. My day."

Her words did what broken glass could not. Pops' anger I could handle. The police I could face. The cousins I could wrangle. But Jessica's disappointment cut deeper than any of it.

Mom pulled her close. Abuela wrapped them both in her shawl. Her friends circled around her, whispering comfort. I stood outside that ring, guilt pressing on my chest like weight I couldn't breathe beneath.

An officer approached, her badge catching the light. "Ramirez," she said, calm but commanding. "We're logging everything. The names help, but we'll still need a full report. Don't touch anything until we finish. Contact the owner. Call your insurance. If you have photos, keep them."

Pops stayed silent, jaw locked. I asked instead—how long would cleanup take, could the paint be stripped before morning, was anything salvageable?

Ramirez shook her head. "Not tonight. We'll give you a case number. The arrogance of tagging names helps you, but this will take time."

Pops shoved a folder into my hands. I crossed to the payphone on the corner. The handset felt cold and sticky, smelling faintly of copper. I left two careful messages for the hall's owner, forcing my tone steady though my stomach churned.

When I returned, Jessica was surrounded again—by friends, by Katy's arm over her shoulder, by the soft murmur of comfort that excluded me.

Inside, the officers worked methodically, their cameras flashing across overturned chairs and ruined decorations. Every burst of light revealed insult layered on sacrifice. Pops measuring walls late at night. Mom sewing fabric at the kitchen table. Abuela humming corridos while folding napkins. All mocked now by paint and cruelty.

Finally Pops spoke, his voice stripped bare. "Do you know how many people are coming tomorrow? One hundred and twenty. If the owner pulls our contract, we lose the hall, the deposit, everything. Your sister wakes up to nothing."

"I know," I said, though the words came thin.

He turned to me. "Fix it."

It wasn't a request. It was a sentence.

Mom stood beside him, one hand on Jessica's back, the other pressed against her mouth to hold in a sob. Abuela's eyes found mine and held steady. "We raised you for storms," she said. "This is only weather. You do not run from weather. You endure it."

"I'm not running," I said, even though part of me wanted to.

Mom's voice was softer, but her meaning sharp. "Then start. She needs a hall tomorrow."

Ramirez returned and handed me a slip of paper with the case number. "We'll patrol. Take care of your family."

I said the plan aloud because speaking made it real: stabilize the hall, salvage what we could, and prepare a backup space before sunrise. Borrow tables from Tío Nacho. Lights from Tía Lupe. Chairs from the community center. A patchwork celebration that might just hold together.

Jessica's eyes filled as she listened. "Fix it," she whispered again. "Please."

"I will," I said, and the words felt like iron.

The hall owner called back near midnight, agreeing to meet us at six. The deposit was gone. Pops made a sound that was half grief, half fury. I touched his arm, not sure whether I was steadying him or myself.

We boarded up windows with cardboard swept glass into piles, took photographs of the wreckage. Katy paged the boys again and again, unanswered signals filling the silence. They were still out there, chasing vengeance that would only make things worse.

Jessica sat wrapped in a blanket in the back seat, Mom smoothing her hair while Abuela stood guard beside them. Her friends whispered prayers. Katy murmured promises. From a distance it looked strong. Up close, it was fragile, ready to break.

I stood by the payphone again, staring down the dark streets where my cousins had vanished. The hall lay ruined. Pops seethed. Jessica's trust cracked in front of me. And all I had was a plan held together by hope and exhaustion.

Leaders don't choose their trials. They rise into them or collapse beneath them.

Years later I told Mack that Shakespeare wrote, "Be not afraid of greatness. Some are born great, some achieve greatness, and some have greatness thrust upon them." That night I stood at the edge of all three, not knowing which one fit, only that the decision would arrive before dawn.

Pops turned to me one last time. His voice was low but steady. "Bring them back. And bring me a hall."
The officers left, taillights fading into the dark. We finished what little could be done—taping, sweeping, locking doors that barely held. Pops drove Mom, Abuela, and Jessica home.

Katy lingered, her hand firm on my shoulder. "You're not alone," she whispered. "But you have to be the one."

When she disappeared into the night, silence filled the parking lot. I climbed into the van, eyes drawn to the names bleeding across the wall. By morning I wanted them erased, buried under music, laughter, and light.

Tonight, all I could see was how close we stood to losing every-thing. I turned the key, the dashboard clock glowing past mid-night, and drove into the dark—balanced between failure and the greatness that had just been forced into my hands.

PRESIDENT BUSH

The night did not quiet when I left the hall; it widened around me, the city inhaling and holding its breath as the van rattled through empty streets. Pops' order sat in my chest beside Jessica's plea, and together they formed a single pulse: bring them back, find a hall, fix it. The weight of it pressed like hands on my shoulders. I told myself to start with what I could control, find the cousins before anger turned into something we couldn't take back.

I didn't need a map to know where they'd gone. When our fury needed space, it always found the park. The place was its own kind of church: chain nets clinking like wind chimes, cracked asphalt under tired sneakers, and streetlights spilling milk-colored halos across the court. I cut the radio, letting the silence settle between engine hums. A siren faded somewhere behind me. A bass line rolled by in the distance and disappeared.

They stood near the sideline in a loose circle. Beto paced like a man trying to walk off lightning. Moi rolled his shoulders, jaw set. Ricky bounced on his heels, pretending to be ready for a fight he didn't want. Jeff lingered a few steps back, eyes on the trees like he was searching for divine permission.

"I swear we find Billy and Erick tonight and make it even," Beto said. His voice cracked through the night like a fuse waiting for spark.

"Even doesn't fix windows," Moi answered, voice low but coiled tight. "Even gets us arrested."

"That wall had names on it," Ricky said. "How stupid do you have to be to tag your own crime?"

Jeff lifted an arm toward a low-hanging branch over the fence. "Forget talking. I'm grabbing this bat."

It wasn't a bat. It was a dead branch, thick at one end and brittle at the other, hanging like it had been waiting for fools. Jeff jumped, caught it, and dangled there kicking wildly, legs flailing like a cartoon drawn too fast. The branch groaned, cracked, and finally gave out, dumping him into the weeds behind the fence.

For a long second, no one breathed. Then Jeff rose from the grass, leaves in his hair and dirt streaked across his cheek, holding the flimsiest stick in San Jose like a weapon forged by destiny. "I'll knock somebody out with this," he declared.

Silence lasted a heartbeat before it collapsed into laughter. Ricky doubled over, Moi covered his face, and Beto nearly fell. "Sit down, President Bush, before you hurt yourself," he gasped between laughs. The nickname hit like a perfect shot. Even Jeff tried to look tough and failed. The stick bent like a fishing pole, and the laughter echoed off the backboards until it felt like the night itself had exhaled.

That was when I heard new footsteps.

Donald approached with his family behind him, an uncle, a few cousins, and a younger sister who looked just like him but carried sharper eyes. The shift in air was instant. Shoulders lifted. Breath shortened. A few steps in either direction could have turned the scene into something worse.

Donald raised his hands. "I didn't touch the hall," he said. "I told Billy and Erick they were idiots for even talking about it. I came here because I heard what happened, and I'm not hiding. I'll say it again if I have to."

Beto crossed his arms. "So why roll in like a parade?"

Donald pointed to the people beside him. "Because my uncle taught me you don't run from mess, you face it. I came to say we weren't part of it, and if you need help cleaning up, we'll show up." His eyes found mine. "You know me, man. You know I'd tell it straight."

Moi stepped forward. "Say it again, looking at him."

Donald didn't blink. "I didn't do it. I told them it was wrong. I'm mad they did it at all."

Before anyone could respond, Jeff lifted his branch. "We can still fight," he announced. No one laughed this time. The air tightened again.

Then everything happened at once.

A car drifted down the street, headlights too high, music too loud, the driver laughing instead of watching the road. Donald's sister, distracted by the noise, took a half step off the curb. Her shoe slid forward just as the bumper veered a little too close. Instinct hit me before thought. I grabbed her arm and yanked hard. The horn screamed. Wind slapped my shoulder. The car brushed past, never slowing.

For a moment the world held its breath again. The branch fell to the dirt. Donald's uncle cursed at the taillights shrinking into the dark. Ricky whispered, "Oh man," over and over. Beto pressed a hand to my shoulder to make sure I was solid.

The girl, Maya, stared at me, her eyes wide and wet, then grabbed my arm like she needed to confirm she was real. Donald pulled her into a hug, looking over her shoulder at me. "That's my sister," he said, voice steady now. "Thank you."

I nodded. "She's okay. That's all that matters."

Beto broke the tension. "President Bush almost took himself out before anybody else."

Jeff tried to glare but smiled instead, tossing the stick aside. "I'm retiring that move."

Laughter rippled again, quieter this time, not wild but human. The air loosened.

Donald faced me. "We'll help you clean," he said. "We'll help you find them if you need that too. But we're not breaking our families over their stupidity."

Maya stepped forward, brushing her hair back. "I'm sorry about the hall," she said. "I don't know your sister, but I know what this night means. My cousin had hers last year. It was every-thing."

Her words landed softly. "Her name's Jessica," I said. "And it's still going to be everything."

Beto kicked the dirt. "So what's the plan?"

"Simple," I said. "We check on the family, meet the owner at six, and rebuild if we have to. If the hall can be saved, we save it. I need every one of you there in the morning."

Jeff nodded, solemn for once. "No more branches."

Ricky raised his hand. "No more bathroom breaks."

Beto smirked. "Do that for the community, man."

Even Maya laughed.

Moi turned to Donald. "If you're serious, be at the lot by eight with people who can lift and people who can listen."

Donald nodded. "We'll be there."

The crowd dissolved slowly, two groups blending into one before heading separate ways. Where the night had felt like a wall, it now looked like a road again. I walked to the van feeling the weight settle differently, less like fear, more like duty. Leadership didn't feel like speeches or titles. It felt like action, movement, and hands on the work.

I told Mack once that Shakespeare said not to fear greatness, some are born great, some achieve greatness, and some have greatness thrust upon them. I didn't feel born for it, and I hadn't achieved it, but the night kept shoving it into my hands. All I could do was hold on.

On the drive back, I cracked the window so my thoughts wouldn't fog the glass. Beto and Ricky whispered jokes to break the quiet. Moi stared at the street ahead like he was memorizing it. Jeff found another leaf in his hair and claimed it was there on purpose.

At a red light, I glanced over at a car full of kids our age, laughing with music shaking their windows. For a heartbeat, I wished our night was that simple. Then the light turned green, and the wish passed.

The lot looked smaller without flashing lights. Pops stood beside his car, contract folder open on the hood. He didn't wave. He waited.

We walked to him in silence. Beto shoved his hands in his pockets. Moi stood beside me. Jeff tried to hide the leaf behind his back. Pops' gaze moved from one face to the next. "You done?" he asked.

"We're with you," I said.

He nodded once. "The owner meets us at six. We won't waste a minute. If you make trouble tonight, stay home tomorrow. If you make work tonight, I'll feed you breakfast."

Ricky muttered, "Work," and Beto echoed, "Breakfast," which almost pulled a smile from Pops before his eyes found the painted wall again. "Go home," he said quietly. "Tomorrow's a long day."

We climbed back into the van, slower now, tired but anchored. I turned the key, and the pager at my hip buzzed. For a second my heart jumped until I looked at the tiny screen, Pops' number and one word, READY.

The message wasn't fancy, but it didn't need to be. It meant be where you said you'd be, bring who you said you'd bring, and make the morning count.

The van rolled forward, and the city finally exhaled. Somewhere, a slow jam floated out of a passing car, and for one brief breath, I thought about Dream Girl and prom and how a weekend could hold love, fear, and hope all at once without breaking. Then the song faded. The road opened.

We would build. We would fix. We would show up.

If greatness had to be thrust upon me, it would find me on time, with my cousins beside me, and a plan that did not let my sister down.

A HALL BY SUNRISE

S leep refused to come that night. Even when I finally stretched out on my bed, my mind spun in endless circles, images of shattered glass, Jessica's stunned face, Pops' clenched jaw. If I did drift off, it was shallow and full of noise. Every creak of the house pulled me back. By the time dawn slid through the blinds, I had stopped pretending to rest. I lay there staring at the ceiling, wondering how to fix what felt unfixable.

At 6:30 sharp, someone knocked at my door. Three steady hits. Not frantic. Not soft. Purposeful. For a second, I thought I was imagining it. Then it came again. I swung my legs off the bed and opened the door, expecting more bad news.

Donald stood there.

Behind him was an older man with silver streaking through dark hair and a face that carried years of both work and wisdom.

Donald's posture was unsure, but his father's presence filled the hallway. He stepped forward before his son could speak.

"This is my father, Juan," Donald said quietly. "He wanted to meet you."

Juan's eyes shone with emotion, the kind that builds before words can catch up. He gripped my hand, strong and deliberate. "You saved my baby girl last night. You saved my Maya." His voice trembled. "How can I ever thank you? Whatever you need, however I can help, I will do it."

The gratitude hit harder than any anger ever could. I tried to wave it off. "Anyone would've done the same."

Juan shook his head. "Not anyone. You did what needed to be done." He took a breath, steady now. "So tell me, mijo, what do you need?"

The answer came out before I even thought about it. "I need a hall," I said. "By tonight."

Juan didn't blink. "Done."

Donald's eyes widened. Relief flashed across his face. Juan nodded once, already moving into action. "Come with me. I have just the place."

Donald hadn't been exaggerating when he said his dad could help. Juan was the manager at the Fairmont Hotel in downtown San Jose, one of the city's crown jewels. Within minutes, he promised us a ballroom big enough to host the entire quinceañera, complete with side rooms for Jessica and her friends to get ready, plus space for our family to breathe and regroup. Overnight, a palace had fallen into our laps. Something beyond what any of us could have dreamed of affording.

I could barely speak. Gratitude filled every part of me, but the words didn't match the size of what he was giving us. I just nodded, thanked him again and again, and finally said, "You and your family have to come tonight. Eat with us. Celebrate with us. That's the least I can do."

I didn't ask my parents first. I didn't have to. Sometimes leadership means doing what feels right before anyone else can question it. That moment taught me that much.

When they left, I stood there for a second, the weight in my chest shifting into something new, responsibility mixed with hope. Then I went to find my parents.

Pops sat on the edge of the bed, elbows on his knees, eyes fixed on the floor. Mom stood near the window, arms folded, still in her robe. The room smelled faintly of coffee and worry. I stopped in the doorway.

"The cousins are safe," I said. "And Pops, I got us a hall."

He looked up slowly. "What did you say?"

"The Fairmont," I said, standing taller now. "Jessica's quince is back on."

For a heartbeat, he didn't move. Then the change came, slow but sure. Pops straightened. His eyes softened. I had seen him proud before, but this was something different. This was respect.

"Mijo," he said quietly, "you're becoming the man I always hoped you'd be."

Mom's eyes shimmered, though she still found her footing. "We're proud of you," she said. "But remember, responsibility doesn't end with tonight. College is still out there waiting."

I smiled. "I know, Mom. I've already started filling out applications. I want the future you both worked for. I'm ready."

Pops rose, his hand heavy on my shoulder but warm. "Go tell your sister," he said. "She needs to hear it from you."

That nearly broke me. I'd rather face the vandals again than the disappointment in Jessica's eyes. Still, I walked to her door and knocked three times.

No answer. Then one of her friends slipped out silently, brushing past me with tear-streaked cheeks. The door stayed half-open. Jessica appeared a moment later, leaning against the frame, arms crossed, eyes sharp.

"What do you want?" she asked.

I took a breath. "To tell you we're good. I found a hall. I've got you, Jess."

She studied me, guarded but curious. "How? How did you even do that?"

I let a small grin slip. "Long story. Maybe one day I'll write it all down, and you can read it. But you'll have to buy the book first."

Her expression cracked just enough for a small smile to break through. "You? A writer? We'll see."

Her voice carried teasing, but something real lived under it. I smiled back. "Yeah. We'll see."

When her door closed, the tension finally eased out of me. For the first time in days, I believed everything might still turn out all right. The story wasn't finished, not even close, but the next chapter finally had a chance to begin.

THE GLOW

By noon the ballroom no longer felt borrowed; it felt claimed. The chandeliers poured warm light across gold trim while round tables stood in perfect ranks, each one dressed with blush napkins, matching plates, and centerpieces rebuilt from the wreckage of the night before. The stage gleamed, the sound check came clean, and the DJ's "one-two" bounced to the ceiling and back, pulling a cheer from the cousins who were ready to celebrate anything that didn't look like disaster.

Before the first guest arrived, the police closed the loop on last night's mess. Billy Ho and Erick had been picked up at dawn, caught mid-excuse with their names still fresh on the wall. The officer told Pops the case was simple, the venue owner was satisfied, and the deposit would be returned in full. Pops listened like a man who had been holding his breath all night and, when the call ended, stepped into the hall, looked to the ceiling, and laughed. A clean, relieved sound that made the rest of us laugh too.

The cousins took the news and ran with it. Jeff staged a fake press conference, Ricky declared a national holiday for "All the Times People Tell on Themselves," and Beto tried out his MC voice: "Erick, that was not vandalism, that was a confession, my guy." Moi shook his head like a man fixing a bad haircut. "Tragic," he said. And it was.

We pivoted from jokes to work, because that's how a Sarabia day moves. The tías floated in with trays and checklists. The Guerrero family arrived with rolled sleeves and easy smiles, blending into the rhythm like they'd always been part of it. Donald kept to the edges at first, but drifted toward Jessica's side of the room when he thought no one saw. He carried garment bags, accepted her quiet thanks, and slipped away again. His silence said everything.

Abuela inspected the room like a general who wins with precision. She straightened a place card, smoothed a tablecloth, and fixed Jeff with a look when he reached for a covered tray. "One," she said, "and use a napkin." Jeff obeyed instantly, took one, used a napkin, and still tried to act like he hadn't licked frosting from his thumb.

The last details slid into place. The court lined up for photos. The DJ shifted from setup tracks to the mix that would carry us through the night, promising cumbias, banda, freestyle, slow jams, and a surprise block he wouldn't name. He grinned like a man who knew how to land a plane in the dark, and I let him keep his secret.

Guests began to fill the space, bringing that soft hum that makes an event real: cousins greeting cousins, kids racing between chairs, aunties comparing outfits and collecting hugs like prizes. Pops stood near the entrance with Mom and Juan, accepting thanks they tried to deflect and passing credit around the circle like pan dulce. For the first time in days, he allowed himself to enjoy being the father of the quinceañera without bracing for another blow.

Then the rear doors opened, and time paused. The chatter fell silent, the kind of hush that feels like the room inhaled all at once. Jessica stood in the doorway.

What she wore rewrote the fairy tale so it belonged to our city. The gown was classic but bold: a fitted bodice that shaped her like it had been drawn for her alone, flowing into a sweeping skirt of layered tulle so light it seemed to breathe. Each step made the fabric ripple like soft water. From her shoulders draped a detachable cape of embroidered tulle that caught the light and fluttered as she turned. The color shimmered between rose gold and sunset, a hue that felt alive, warm, and luminous under the chandeliers. Hidden beneath the skirt, a lattice of tiny LED lights waited quietly, ready to wake later when the baile sorpresa called for stars.

For one heartbeat, the room forgot to move. Then the applause came in waves. Moi whispered, "She's not walking, she's floating." Beto clutched his chest. "Princess, but the kind who can roast." Ricky blinked. "Is anyone else seeing the glow, or did my horchata betray me?" Katy smiled. She didn't need to say anything.

The ceremony unfolded with the gravity of tradition and the joy of survival. Mom and Abuela presented the last doll, a tiny version of Jessica's dress. Pops traded her flats for heels that caught and scattered the light, his pride wordless but visible. The tiara settled perfectly into place, and when the court gathered for the waltz, every step fell in rhythm like they'd practiced for a life-time.

Then the music shifted. The surprise dance began, and the hidden lights bloomed under Jessica's skirt, turning her gown into a constellation. The room erupted. Tías shouted blessings, kids screamed, and the DJ laughed into the mic. "Okay, princesa," he said. "Take your moment." She did. She owned it.

The cousins turned the dance floor into theater. Jeff tried a dramatic dip and almost dropped his partner; she laughed first, which saved him. Ricky attempted a moonwalk and lost to friction. Moi was flawless, drawing a small circle of awe until Beto began narrating like a fight announcer. One sharp cough from Abuela brought them all back to order. Katy guided a line of younger primitas with the calm authority of a teacher who didn't need volume to control a room.

Between dances, our families stitched themselves together. The Guerreros told stories about Maya and Donald, and the Sarabias answered with stories about Jessica and me. Someone discovered both families had kids who went to the same elementary school years apart. Someone else realized Juan knew the chef at Pops' favorite taquería. The connections stacked easily until the room felt less like two families meeting and more like one reuniting after time apart.

Dinner arrived in waves: rice light as air, beans with a slow burn, trays of mole that tasted like home, tamales vanishing faster than lids could close, and a tres leches cake crowned with strawberries. Plates returned empty, laughter grew louder, and even the teasing softened. Every sound carried gratitude.

When our brother-sister dance began, nerves that had survived everything else tried to rise again. Jessica placed her hand in mine, and for a moment, the noise of the world fell away. We moved slowly, turning with the rhythm that had shaped our whole childhood.

"Thank you," she said. "You were the hero I always knew you could be. Remember this: a hero is made in the moment, not by questioning the past or fearing what's ahead." She smiled so I wouldn't fall apart.

It took me a turn to find my voice. "I've got your back," I said. "Always." The words didn't feel new, they felt remembered.

Later, under the glow of the last songs, I watched Donald and Jessica trade a few quiet smiles. No fireworks, no big declarations. Just small kindnesses, a glass of water, a laugh, a gentle step around her dress. It was enough. Maybe even the start of something.

Near midnight, the DJ leaned into the mic one last time. "This one's for the families still on their feet," he said. Then came the slow jams, the dedications, the warmth of songs that feel like a benediction. Couples swayed. Abuela pretended to scold Beto, then laughed when he bowed for a dance. The room didn't dim; it deepened.

Hours slipped by. Shoes came off. Ties hung loose. Pops tried to leave twice, but the tías pulled him back. Mom's smile never faded. Juan looked around the room like a man who'd witnessed a promise fulfilled. The cousins danced until even their jokes ran out of energy.

By four in the morning, we drifted from the ballroom, the air outside cool and soft with relief. We gathered our things, accepted hugs, and rode the elevator up to the rooms Juan had given us. One by one, doors clicked shut down the hall, a quiet percussion marking the end of the night.

I thought the story was finished. I set my pager on the nightstand, took off my shoes, and reached for the lamp. Sleep waited just ahead. Then came a knock at my door, soft, careful, deliberate, the kind that says the story isn't over yet.

HOW IT ENDS AND BEGINS AGAIN

The suite was quiet except for the city breathing beyond the glass. I had barely set my bag down when there was a knock at the door. Through the peephole, I saw Jessica's quiet friend, the one who always seemed to fade into the background yet carried herself with an unmistakable elegance. I opened the door and asked if everything was good. She nodded nervously and asked if I had a minute. I stepped aside and let her in.

She drifted toward the balcony, hands clasped, moving with a grace that felt both unsure and inevitable. "I hope you don't mind," she said softly. "I've never seen the city from this perspective." She lifted her hands and framed the skyline with her fingers like she was capturing a scene for a film. I chuckled and said, "I didn't think I'd see it like this either. These rooms are expensive." She giggled, the sound breaking the tension. "Well, you did get the hook up." We both laughed, and the air loosened.

Finally, I asked what was up. She turned to me, a little braver now. "You know this almost all went off the rails this weekend."

"Yeah," I said, shaking my head. "If it wasn't one thing, it was another."

She studied me with warmth. "You did amazing."

I smiled. "Thank you. But I'd do anything for my sister. Is that why you're here? Just to thank me?"

She shook her head. "No. I had a question."

"Okay, fire away."

"Do you have a date for the prom?"

I froze, heart pounding, then smiled. "Are you asking me, or are you collecting chisme for someone else?"

She tilted her head, eyes steady. "I'm asking you, silly."

I stared at her, pulse racing. "Gaby... it's literally the one thing I wanted this weekend."

Her eyebrows lifted. "So you do know my name."

I laughed nervously. "Of course I do. You've been my dream girl for a long time."

She smiled, the kind that reached her eyes. "Sometimes dreams become reality."

She stepped closer. I leaned in, and our first kiss felt like the start of everything.

When the balcony blurred, the present day returned. I was back in Mack's room, the fans still humming from cleanup, the smell of damp carpet fading. Mack looked at me, wide-eyed. "So Dream Girl was Mom the whole time?"

Gaby raised her hand like a guilty student. "That's me." The three of us laughed, and the secret became family history.

A knock on the door pulled us back. Jessica entered, carrying a long garment bag. With her usual mix of confidence and precision, she unzipped it to reveal a sweep of rose-gold tulle. "My quince dress," she said. "It survived once; it can survive again if you want it, Mack."

Mack gasped. Jessica smiled, firm as always. "We can pin and hem it in an hour. We're Sarabias, we make it work." The room shifted from worry to purpose.

The ballroom gleamed that night. Candlelight sparkled in glass centerpieces. Music pulsed through the air. Family poured in, their laughter and voices layering into the rhythm of the evening.

Ricky arrived first, chest out, carrying a gift and business cards that read Sarabia Sanitation. He grinned and declared, "People always need bathrooms. I just made it an empire." We cracked up, but we were proud. Ricky had turned his infamous emergencies into a business that thrived across the Bay.

Jeff followed in a sharp suit that screamed boardroom. He clasped my hand and boomed, "Still the president. President

Bush, forever." We all laughed at the memory of him swinging a tree branch like a weapon, but truth was, Jeff had built a company in San Francisco and wore the title proudly. The roast would last forever, but so would the respect.

Moi walked in smooth as ever, tie perfectly knotted, comb still in his pocket. But this time, his swagger came with substance. He was a sports agent now, representing athletes we watched on TV. "Courtside seats next month," he whispered to me. "Don't embarrass me on the Jumbotron." He winked, still convinced he was the smoothest man alive, but we knew he earned his place.

Beto arrived loud, roasting everyone within earshot, claiming Walmart ran smoother because of him. He still talked faster than anyone could keep up with, still lived for the roast, but behind it he had built a career as a regional manager. He lowered his volume when Abuela appeared, kissed her cheek, and hauled chairs like muscle for the family. Beneath the noise, there was always love.

Robert came next, quieter than the others. His smile was small but genuine as he hugged me. Robert had stumbled plenty, in and out of jail, trying to climb uphill. But he was climbing, and every time we saw him, we rooted for him like he was taking the last shot of the game. His presence was a victory in itself.

Katy swept in with glitter wrapping on her gift. She hugged Mack, looked her in the eyes, and told her she was perfect. Katy had grown into a kindergarten teacher, still wielding her wit like a weapon, but now using it to guide little ones. She kept us in line then, and she kept her students in line now.

Jessica managed the night with the precision of a general. She had become a lawyer, no surprise to anyone. She carried herself with authority, but tonight she was also just a sister, watching Mack step into a tradition she herself had lived years before.

And Gaby, my Dream Girl, had gone from prom date to wife to filmmaker. She moved through the room with a camera on her shoulder, catching the glow of family, laughter, and love. Her own stories reached audiences now, but she never stopped holding onto the truth and the light.

As for me, I finally accepted the title I had been circling since those days in the van. I became an author. Turns out all this chisme, all this chaos, all this love, it was material. It was memory. It was who we were.

The quinceañera unfolded in all its glory. Mack accepted the last doll, changed into her new shoes, and wore Jessica's gown like it had been waiting just for her. Our father-daughter dance slowed the room to a heartbeat. She whispered to me, "A hero is made in the moment." Words Jessica once told me, words I had carried, now passed on to her.

The cousins partied late into the night, joined by the Guerreros. Donald shook my hand, his family laughing alongside ours. The music roared, the dance floor burned, and by the time we finally retired to our suites, it was four in the morning. None of us cared.

Before lights dimmed, I stood for one last look. Ricky worked a deal by the punch bowl. Jeff made toasts as if campaigning. Moi fielded calls between songs. Beto roasted until his voice cracked, then carried boxes. Robert sat with Abuela, laughing at something only he could see. Katy lined up little cousins like students on a field trip. Jessica moved like a force of nature, keeping it all together. And Gaby, my Gaby, filmed it all, turning family into story.

And me? I stood with notebook in hand, ready to write it down, because chisme isn't just gossip. It's how we tell the truth about who we are, with laughter, with tears, with love strong enough to survive broken halls and long nights.

Some are born great. Some achieve greatness. And some have greatness thrust upon them. For me, it was never about which one I was. It was about showing up exactly when the story needed me to. That night, I did. And now, mija, this is how it ends, and how it begins again.

ACKNOWLEDGEMENTS

First, to **Jackson**, my little chaos goblin. You were the spark for this whole thing when you told me you wanted to read one of my books in school. That moment lit a fire in me. You inspire me more than you realize, and I hope you laugh reading this as much as I laughed writing it...because a lot of these pages are straight-up chaos.

Mackenzie, you are low-key the heart of this book. Being the only teenager I had around meant you were automatically cast, but the truth is you made the perfect model. The book version of Mack is built on who you are: smart, funny, strong, and just a little too good at roasting me. You are a fantastic young lady, and I am proud of the person you are becoming.

To **Gaby**, thank you for being the blueprint for the book's Gaby. I needed a strong Latina character and you gave me plenty to work with. You're quick, funny, and have a talent for reminding me that no story or bad joke gets past you without commentary. Half our conversations at work already feel like scenes out of this book, so it only made sense. Thanks for being a friend who can roast me one minute and hype me up the next.

To **Katy**: thank you for trusting me with a piece of your name and a sliver of your spirit. Letting me fold that into the book made the character truer and kinder than I could have written on my own. You are the best internet friend I have ever met.

To **Gulraj and Amri**, thank you for being kind, patient, and letting me use work hours like my own personal writer's lounge. Every time I came in with some half-baked idea, you listened. That support has meant more than you know.

And finally, to all the people who inspired the stories woven into these pages. Some of your names made it in, some did not, but you know who you are. Growing up in San Jose was a gift. I carry the memories with me: the roasts, the all-day basketball games, the carne asada cookouts, the parties, the late nights, the game sessions that always ended in someone getting roasted the hardest. Those moments, and all of you, gave me the heart of this book.

Sergio Serna is a storyteller who writes with equal parts heart, humor, and honesty. His work centers Latino culture, family, and the everyday moments that shape us.

He is the author of *One Nation: The Untold Story of Raider Nation*, a book that celebrates the passion and loyalty of Raiders fans across generations and cities, and the *¡Viva los Sueños!* series, which introduces children to Latino trailblazers and everyday heroes. His most recent work, *10 CDs for a Penny: Growing Up Gen X with Bruises, Burnt Pop-Tarts, and Zero Therapy*, is an unapologetic, hilarious, and heartfelt memoir of survival, nostalgia, and the chaos of coming of age in the Gen X era.

With *That Quince Weekend*, Sergio expands his voice into the world of young adult fiction, blending his gift for cultural storytelling with the humor and chaos of family life. His writing breaks stereotypes, uplifts community, and proves that Latino stories belong on every shelf.

Sergio lives in California with his family, where he continues to write, create, and champion stories that celebrate culture, memory, and identity.

THAT QUINCE WEEKEND